KU-024-038

WILLIMENA RULES!

RULE BOOK #4
How to (Almost) Ruin Your School Play

By Valerie Wilson Wesley
Illustrated by Maryn Roos

JUMP AT THE SUN
HYPERION BOOKS FOR CHILDREN • NEW YORK

For Jackie, always a star

If you purchased this book without a cover, you should be aware that this book is stolen property. It was reported as "unsold and destroyed" to the publisher, and neither the author nor the publisher has received any payment for this "stripped" book.

Text copyright © 2005 by Valerie Wilson Wesley
Illustrations copyright © 2005 by Maryn Roos

All rights reserved. No part of this book may be reproduced or transmitted in any form or by any means, electronic or mechanical, including photocopying, recording, or by any information storage and retrieval system, without written permission from the publisher.
For information address Hyperion Books for Children, 114 Fifth Avenue, New York, New York 10011-5690.

Printed in the United States of America

First Edition

3 5 7 9 10 8 6 4 2

Library of Congress Cataloging-in-Publication Data on file.

ISBN 0-7868-5259-3

Visit www.jumpatthesun.com

My Rules Step by Step

Willimena's Rules

STEP #1:
Have a Playwright for a Sister

Sometimes my sister, Tina, gets all the breaks. For one thing, she's two years older than me, so she's taller and can reach things I can't. She also knows how to write cursive and multiply fractions. Most of the time, I'm not jealous of her, but sometimes I just can't help it. Like the other night at dinner, when she made her big announcement.

"Guess what, everybody!" she said as she twirled spaghetti onto her fork.

1

"My play, *The Terrific Tale of Tara, the Proud Fairy Princess*, won the school playwriting contest." Tina's grin was one of the biggest I'd ever seen on her face.

My dad put down his fork. My mom put down her glass. Even Doofus Doolittle, our cat and one of my best friends, gave a loud meow.

"That's terrific!" said my dad.

"Congratulations, Tina! I'm so proud of you," said my mom.

Doofus Doolittle jumped into Tina's lap. He put his chin next to hers and licked sauce off her cheek. Tina gave him a hug. Then she looked at me. I could see she was happy. I knew she was waiting for me to say something nice, too.

"That's great, Tina," I said. "That's good news!"

Now, don't get me wrong. I *really* did mean it. I *really* was happy for Tina. I had a *really* big smile on my face. But there was a teeny-weeny, itsy-bitsy spot inside of me that didn't mean it all *that* much.

"And guess what else, everybody! Guess what else!" Tina said. "I get to help Mrs. White direct the play and decide who will be in it."

"We're so happy for you!" my mom and dad said together, like they were the same person.

"What are the roles?" asked my dad.

"Well, there's Max, the wise giant, who is big and tall. He's the oldest person in the play," said Tina. "There are four elves, who are tiny and cute. Igor is the mean, evil prince, who does bad things, and there's the star of the play. Her name is

Tara, and she is the proud fairy princess. There are also a lot of trees."

"Trees? How come there are trees in your play?" Putting trees in a play sounded dumb to me, but I didn't say it. Trees are usually painted on the back of the stage. They're just scenery.

"I wanted a lot of kids to be in my play, so I made the trees characters," Tina said.

"That was such a good idea," said my dad.

"What a thoughtful thing to do!" said my mom.

Doofus Doolittle rubbed up against Tina and purred.

"Who would want to play a dumb tree?" I said.

Tina looked hurt. "Lots of kids."

"What do the trees say?"

"Nothing, of course. They're trees! That's a dumb question, Willie. Have you ever heard a tree talk?"

Suddenly, the *old* Tina was back. That's the Tina who reminds me she's my older sister. The one who bosses me around and likes to get her way.

"Don't call me dumb, Tina!" I said. "It's dumb to have a dumb play with a bunch of dumb trees standing around!"

My mom and dad looked at each other. Then they looked at me and Tina.

"Girls, don't start calling each other names," my mom said.

"I don't want any fighting tonight," my dad said.

"She started it by saying my play was dumb," Tina said. I could tell she was hurt.

I was sorry I had said it. But I wasn't ready to tell Tina yet.

"But you called me dumb," I said instead.

"Apologize," my mom said.

"Her first," Tina said.

"Sorry," I said.

"Me, too," said Tina. Nobody spoke for a while. Even Doofus Doolittle was quiet.

Finally, my mom asked, "Can everybody in the whole school try out for the play?"

"Anybody who is a good actor."

"Willie is a very good actor!" my dad said. "Remember when Willie was the frog in that play a few years back?"

"Yes, she was great!" my mom added.

"She was the best frog I ever saw," Tina said. I knew she was trying to make up. My whole family was trying to make me feel better. I tried to smile, but somehow it just wouldn't come. For one thing, the frog play had happened a long time ago. I was in kindergarten, and all I had to do was sit, croak, and pretend to catch flies.

"You were *so* cute with your green face and green tights," my mom said with a smile.

"And you certainly did some of the best croaking I've ever heard!" added my dad.

"I was so proud of you!" Tina said.

There are times when your family knows just what to say to make you feel better. *This* was not one of those times.

My dad turned back to Tina. "So who do you want to be in your play?"

"Well," Tina said in a serious voice, "the giant has to be one of the sixth graders because he or she has to be bigger than anybody else. The cute little elves will be in kindergarten or first grade. Igor, the evil prince, should probably be a boy, but a girl can play him, too. And of course the best part, the part of Tara, the proud fairy princess, will have to be someone who is very, very special."

"I'll bet every girl in the whole school will want to play that part," my mom said.

"Mrs. White said we should choose a girl in the third grade."

Third grade? That was *my* grade!

"The proud fairy princess is very smart but sometimes she gets into trouble. She's a good person, but sometimes she does the wrong thing. She tries to help people, but sometimes she gets them into more trouble. But her heart is always in the right place. Her one fault is that she's very proud."

Except for the proud stuff, Tara sounded like somebody I knew.

Me!

Without even reading Tina's play, I knew the role I wanted, and I was sure I couldn't miss. Even though Tina and I fought a lot, when things were bad, she was always in my corner. I could usually count on her to help me out when I needed it most. There were times when my sister could turn into my very best friend. A smile spread across my face. Suddenly I knew that things would be all right. With my sister's help, I could hop from frog to fairy princess in one short lifetime!

STEP #2:
Beg for the Starring Role

Before I got dressed for bed that night, I wrote in my journal:

I hope I will be the star of Tina's play.

I wrote it ten times down the middle of the page. I didn't know if that would do any good, but I thought I'd try it anyway. Then I remembered what my grandma said about positive thinking. Positive thinking means believing that the *best* will happen instead of the *worst*.

So I crossed out "I hope" on the page and drew a line under *will*. Now it read:

~~I hope~~ I WILL be the star of Tina's play.

That felt better.

After my mom turned out the lights, I said to Tina, "I *really* want to be the proud fairy princess in your play."

Tina didn't answer.

"Did you hear me?" I sat up and looked over at her bed. She had pulled the blanket over her head. She does that when she doesn't want to talk.

"Please, Tina. With chocolate sprinkles on top."

Tina pulled down her blanket. She climbed out of her bed and sat down on mine. When she put her arm around me,

I got a bad feeling. Tina only does that when she is about to tell me something I don't want to hear.

"Willie, I can't pick you to be the star just because you're my sister," she said.

"But kids pick best friends to do special stuff all the time, and being sisters is better than being best friends. It's *your* play. Why can't you do it?"

"It wouldn't be fair. You have to try out like everybody else."

"But what if I don't get the part I want?"

"Well, a lot of kids won't get the parts they want."

"But I really want it, and I know I'm the best person."

"A lot of kids think they're the best person," Tina said.

"Can't you just help me a little bit," I said. "We *are* sisters! Please? Please? Please?"

I can count on two fingers the number of times I've begged Tina for something. Twice. The first time was three years ago when I begged her to give me a ride on her new bike. The second time was six months ago when I asked her not to tell Mom I broke her blue glass vase. Neither time worked.

"That wouldn't be fair, Willie." Tina's voice was serious. I knew she meant it.

"Please, Tina!" This would be the third time. It really hurt.

Tina sighed a heavy sigh.

"You are my sister, I guess," she said, like maybe she wasn't so sure about it. "I'll tell you what I'm going to do." She turned

13

on the lamp near her bed and went into her backpack. She pulled out a blue folder marked THE TERRIFIC TALE OF TARA, THE PROUD FAIRY PRINCESS and gave it to me.

"This is a copy of my play. Mrs. White gave me an extra one when she ran it off this afternoon. I'm going to give it to you so you can have a head start rehearsing for the role. I guess that will be okay. But don't tell anyone, and don't ask me for anything else!"

"Thank you, Tina. Thank you so much! I'm going to work really hard. I hope I get it! I hope I do!"

"Don't worry, Willie. You'll do fine!" Tina said.

I gave my sister a big hug. Then I put *The Terrific Tale of Tara, the Proud Fairy Princess* under my pillow. Maybe the words would creep into my head while I slept.

The next day at school, Mrs. Sweetly gave all the kids in my class a copy of Tina's play.

"I want you all to read and study the part you want to play," she said. "Everyone will have a chance to try out."

I was proud to see Tina's name on the cover. It made me glad that Tina was my sister. But I could always count on Crawford Mills to turn my pride into pain.

"Tina Thomas! Isn't that silly Willie Thomas's crazy sister?" he cried out. Everybody started to laugh.

"I hate you, Crawford Mills!" I whispered to myself.

"Crawford, I don't want to hear that!" said Mrs. Sweetly with a scowl. She stood up and shook her finger at Crawford Mills.

He sank down into his seat. That made me feel better. "Willie should be very proud of her sister, and I'm sure she is. Tina Thomas has written a very good play."

Mrs. Sweetly wrote in big letters on the blackboard:

PLAY TRYOUTS NEXT MONDAY!

I opened my copy of Tina's play and imagined myself dressed as Tara, the proud fairy princess.

Everybody in my class was excited about the play and wanted to be in it. Mrs. Sweetly said that we should all try out for all the roles. Most of the girls wanted to play Tara, the proud fairy princess. Most of the boys wanted to play Igor, the mean, evil prince.

Every chance I got, I tried to memorize Princess Tara's lines. I'd read them out loud, then close my eyes and try to see the words in my mind. Then I'd say them out loud again. I whispered them to myself while I rode the bus to school. I practiced them when I ate my lunch. I sang them in the tub as I took my bath. I wrote them down before I went to bed at night.

Most of the lines in the play were spoken by Princess Tara and Prince Igor. Max, the wise giant, and the cute little elves didn't have much to say. The trees, which included saplings, weeping willows, and oaks, just stood on stage. Princess Tara and Prince Igor talked mostly to each other. I had to learn Igor's lines so I could learn Tara's. By the end of the week, I practically knew the whole play by heart.

On Saturday morning, all the kids on my block gathered in the Greenes' backyard like we did every Saturday. But things were different this time. We weren't just there to play. Next Monday we would be competing in the big tryouts. All the kids

who went to my school wanted a role in Tina's play.

When Tina and I walked into the Greenes' backyard everybody crowded around us. It was like we were giving away chocolate-chip cookies.

"Tina, you wrote the best play I've ever read," said Gregory Greene. He was trying out for the part of Max, the wise giant.

"You're so lucky that Tina is your big sister. I wish I had a sister like Tina," said Pauline. She was trying out for Princess Tara.

Even Betty and Booker, the youngest kids on our block, got into the act. They were trying out for the parts of the cute little elves.

"Tina, I saved this for you from lunch," said Betty as she handed Tina a peppermint lollipop.

"I made this for you at school," said Booker. He gave Tina a card covered with her name surrounded by blue and silver stars.

Everybody was treating Tina like she

was a big-time movie star because they wanted her to choose them.

It was disgusting!

"Thank you, everybody. Thank you all so much," said Tina, as if she were on TV. She popped the lollipop into her mouth and handed me Booker's card.

"Hold this for me, Willie," she said, as if I were her servant.

"Don't boss me around, Tina! Hold it yourself!" I said.

"You shouldn't talk to your big sister like that, silly Willie," said Crawford Mills. He was trying out for the part of Igor, the mean, evil prince.

"Mind your own business, Crawford," I said.

"Children, children, let's have some peace!" Tina said, sounding like a grown-up.

She even looked like she'd grown a couple of inches.

"You are all my dear friends, and I'd just like to wish everyone here the very best of luck on Monday in the big tryout! You all have my best wishes. All I can say is: have fun, everyone, and may the best actors win."

She blew everybody a kiss. Then she took a bow.

I couldn't believe what I was seeing. Winning that contest had gone straight to my sister's head. But the crazy part was, everybody started to clap!

At the end of the day, though, I was no better than anybody else.

"Tina, *please, please* stick up for me when I try out for Princess Tara on Monday!" I said before we went to sleep. After the way everybody had acted in the Greenes' backyard, I thought a little more begging might improve my chances.

As usual, Tina didn't answer. Maybe she didn't hear me. Or maybe she just didn't want to.

STEP #3:
A. Borrow Your Sister's Lucky Charm
B. Lose Your Sister's Lucky Charm

"Can I borrow the good-luck charm Teddy gave you?" I asked Tina on Monday morning. Teddy is our cousin. His good-luck charm is a four-leaf clover in a plastic case. The last time Teddy visited us, the charm had brought him good luck. It helped him catch a big fish. Maybe it would help me "catch" the role of Tara, the proud fairy princess.

Tina looked doubtful. "I might need it myself."

"You've already had good luck. You won the play contest!"

"Why don't you wear your lucky red socks?"

"I have them on, but I need a double dose," I said.

"Don't you dare lose it," Tina said as she gave me it to me. I could tell she really didn't want to do it. I knew how important it was to her, and I wondered if I should take it. But I needed every bit of luck I could get.

"I promise to keep it safe."

"You'd better," Tina said in a scary voice. Her eyes were narrow. Her lips were tight. It was Tina's meanest look. There

26

was no telling what she would do to me if I lost it. Tina had glued a safety pin on the back of her charm so she could wear it on her clothes instead of carrying it. I pinned the charm on my purple sweater. It looked a little weird, but I didn't care. I just hoped it would do its job.

When I walked into my class, everybody was gathered in the front of the room.

TRYOUTS FOR MAJOR CHARACTERS THIS AFTERNOON! was written in big letters on the blackboard.

Nearly all the kids in my class were excited about trying out for the play. Everyone was talking at once.

"Sit down now, boys and girls!" said Mrs. Sweetly. "We have work to do today. The children who want to try out for the play will go to the auditorium after lunch."

The morning seemed to go on forever. Everything was in slow motion. It took one kid an hour to read a sentence. Even simple stuff like adding 25 and 10 took forever to do. When Mrs. Sweetly asked for the capital of the United States, somebody said it was New York City. Everybody was like me—too nervous to think straight.

After lunch, Mrs. Sweetly gave the kids who wanted to try out for the play a pass to go to the auditorium.

"My last name is Starr, and I know I'm going to be Tara, the proud fairy princess," said Lilac Starr. She was first in line. Some people think Lilac will grow up to be a movie star. Last year, she got more Valentine's Day cards than anybody else in the whole second grade. But a lot of kids say she's stuck-up. Sometimes she's nice to me, like when my mom puts extra cookies in my lunch bag. Most of the time she's not.

"I hope I get the part of Igor, the mean, evil prince," said Bill Taylor. He had his fingers crossed like I did.

Crawford Mills didn't say anything. He just looked down at his feet.

I was surprised that Crawford Mills was trying out for the play. It didn't seem like something he'd want to do.

"Good luck, Willie," he muttered as we walked to the auditorium. That surprised me, too.

When we came into the auditorium, each class sat in a different row. Betty and Booker and the other kids from kindergarten and first grade were in the front row. They were all trying out for cute little elves. Kids in the third grade, like me, who were trying out for Tara and Igor, were in the second row. There were only about four sixth graders trying out for Max, the wise giant. One was Gregory Greene. When he saw me he waved, and I waved back.

At first, I didn't see Tina and Mrs. White, but then I spotted Tina in the last row. She grinned and gave me the *okay* sign. That made me feel good. It meant my sister was rooting for me.

Mrs. White came to the front of the room and climbed up on the stage. "I hope that everybody has been studying hard," she said. "This afternoon we will have try-outs. Tomorrow we will announce over the PA system who got the parts."

Everybody in the room clapped when she said that.

"I would like all the people who are trying out to come onstage. To help you get into character, I have costumes that I want each of you to wear when you read or recite your lines."

The costumes for the cute little elves were bright red-and-orange stocking caps. The one for Max, the wise giant, was a black wooden cane. Igor, the mean, evil prince, wore a cardboard crown made of daggers. A grin spread across my face when I saw the costume for Tara. It was a long, blue velvet cape with white lace on the edges. I could hardly wait to put it on.

I could see that Booker and Betty were nervous when they came onstage. Booker put his cap on backward. Everybody laughed except me. I knew how he felt. I wondered how he would feel if his sister got a part in the play and he didn't. I knew he would be happy for her. But I also knew there might be a teeny-weeny spot inside of him that would be jealous, too.

Finally it was time for the third graders. The boys who wanted to play Igor had to go first. Everyone did a good job. But Crawford Mills was the only boy who knew all the lines. He must have been studying as hard as I had. I wondered if he knew Tara's lines as well as I knew Igor's.

Because Lilac Starr's name begins with an S and mine begins with a T, she tried out first. When she came up on the stage, she walked very slowly, like she had all the time in the world. It was as if she expected everyone to wait for her. She held her head high. She looked straight ahead, like she didn't want to see any-

body. When she picked up the blue cape, she tossed it around her shoulders like it belonged to her. I smiled to myself. There was no way Lilac Starr would get the part. She was acting too stuck-up.

Then it was my turn.

When somebody in a cartoon gets scared, their knees shake. They can't swallow. Their lips won't move. Once upon a time, I laughed when that happened to cartoon people. Never again! That was how I felt when it was my turn. I was so scared, I couldn't move.

"Willie Thomas!" I heard somebody say. "Is Willie Thomas here?"

I couldn't answer. I couldn't move my feet. Then Crawford gave me a shove, and the next thing I knew, I was standing right in the middle of the stage. I didn't know whether to thank Crawford or yell at him.

"Are you ready, Willie?" asked Mrs. White.

"Yes," I said. Then my mind went blank.

"Maybe you should put on the cape," she said.

I took off my sweater and slipped on the

34

cape. I pulled the cape around me. I closed my eyes. The first line of the play was said by Prince Igor. When I said his first line to myself, all the others suddenly came back. Somehow, I got them all out.

I tried not to look at anybody when I went back to my seat.

"That was good, Willie!" Betty and Booker said together as I passed their row.

I couldn't believe what I was hearing. Were they teasing me?

"You did okay!" Gregory said with a wink on his way to the stage.

When the tryouts were over and we were going back to class, Tina ran over and gave me a hug. Even Crawford Mills gave me a pat on my back.

Suddenly I felt better. Maybe I hadn't been so bad, after all. Maybe I had just imagined the worst. The good-luck charm must have worked.

That was when I remembered my sweater. I must have left it on the stage! I broke out of line and ran back into the auditorium. I didn't care if I got into trouble. I climbed onto the stage and looked around for it. But my sweater, with Tina's good-luck charm pinned on it, was gone.

STEP #4:
If YOUR Part Goes to a Stuck-up Kid—Make Like a Tree and LEAVE!

Wherever it was, the good-luck charm was working. Luck was with me when I got home from school. Tina was so excited about her play, she forgot to ask me what had happened to it. She did all the talking during dinner, mostly about her play. I didn't have much to say. It was Tina's night to do the dishes, so after I did my homework, I took my bath early and went straight to bed.

"Are you feeling okay, Willie? You hardly said anything during dinner," my mom asked when she came to kiss me good night. I could tell she was worried.

"I'm fine, Mom. I'm just tired," I said, faking a yawn.

"Well, try to get a good night's sleep. Tomorrow you'll find out if you'll be playing Tara, the proud princess."

When Tina came into the room, I closed my eyes tight.

"Willie, are you still awake?" Tina asked from her bed.

I pretended to be asleep. I was afraid she would ask about her good-luck charm. The next morning, I got up before Tina, ate my breakfast fast, and got on the bus before Tina did. Tina likes to sit in the back of the bus. I sat behind the bus driver. When the bus reached the school, I jumped off the moment it stopped and ran straight to the Lost and Found in the principal's office. My fingers were crossed the whole time.

"My, Willie, you've come in bright and early," said Mrs. Morris, the principal. "You must have lost something very important to come to the Lost and Found this early in the day." Mrs. Morris pulled out a large cardboard box marked LOST AND FOUND. The box was crammed to the top with junk. There were at least fifty mismatched gloves and mittens. Most of them had holes. There were about twenty broken barrettes and a long, red-and-white-striped scarf. Pushed into one corner was a teddy bear with a torn ear. It made me sad to see him there. If I hadn't

been so worried about Tina's good-luck
charm, I would have asked Mrs. Morris
where he would go if nobody claimed him.
I would have loved to take him home. But
I was too worried to think about that now.

"What are you looking so hard for,

Willie? Maybe I can help you," Mrs. Morris said.

"My purple sweater."

"So many children forget sweaters, I have a special box just for those." She went into her office and came back with a plastic box filled with neatly folded sweaters. I spotted mine right on top. I was saved! I pulled it out and quickly slipped it on. But Tina's good-luck charm wasn't where I'd pinned it. All that was left were two tiny pinholes.

"Oh, no!" I said, pointing to the spot where it had been pinned. "I had a good-luck charm right here!"

"Was it pinned to your sweater?" Mrs. Morris asked. I could tell she was concerned. "The safety pin must have popped open, and it must have fallen off," she said.

All I could do was nod. I was afraid to trust my voice. Tina's lucky charm could be anywhere in the school. Chances were I'd never find it again.

I went back to Mrs. Sweetly's class with my head hanging low. Could things get any worse?

You bet they could.

I was so worried about losing Tina's good-luck charm, I'd almost forgotten that Mrs. White would make an announcement about the roles in Tina's play. At the end of the day, her voice boomed out over the PA system.

"Attention, all children who tried out for roles in *The Terrific Tale of Tara, the Proud Fairy Princess*," she said.

All the kids stopped what they were doing. Everybody looked up at the speaker as if Mrs. White was going to step out of it. For three minutes, I actually forgot about Tina's good-luck charm. I could see myself onstage, wrapped in Tara's cape, smiling down at the audience. I could see myself taking bows. I could hear the applause.

My happiness lasted for exactly 180 seconds. I know, because somewhere inside my head, I counted every measly one. That was how long it took Mrs. White to announce who got the roles.

She started with the youngest kids. I guess she didn't want to keep them waiting.

"The roles of the four cute little elves will be played by Jennifer Greene, Ford Baldwin, and Booker and Betty Carter," Mrs. White said.

"That's great! That's great!" I screamed out loud. I had a big grin on my face. I was so glad for Booker and Betty, I wanted to stand up and cheer.

"The part of Igor, the mean evil prince, will be played by Crawford Mills, from Mrs. Sweetly's third-grade class," said Mrs. White.

"Wow!" Crawford said. "I got it! I got it!"

Everybody started to clap. Everyone was happy for Crawford, even me. Secretly, though, I wished that another kid had gotten the role. As Tara, the proud fairy princess, I wasn't looking forward to spending a lot of time talking to Crawford Mills.

"And Mrs. Sweetly must have some very good actors in her class," continued Mrs. White. "Bill Taylor will be Crawford's understudy. That means that he will play the role if Crawford can't.

"And we have yet another member of Mrs. Sweetly's class who will be in the play," Mrs. White continued.

My heart jumped. I tried to keep my lips from trembling. Sometimes that happens when my smile gets too big.

"The role of Tara, the proud fairy princess, will be played by Lilac Starr."

I couldn't believe my ears! I sat stiff in my chair, too shocked to move. How could this happen? Mrs. White read out who would play the part of Lilac's understudy, but I didn't even hear it.

"I knew I would probably get it!" I heard Lilac say to the kid sitting next to her. "I usually get what I want."

Of all the kids who tried out for the role, why did it have to go to Lilac Starr? Wasn't it enough that she got more cards

The role of Tara, the proud fairy princess, will be played by Lilac Starr.

than anybody else on Valentine's Day? And now she was getting the role of a lifetime! The one I was supposed to play. How unfair could life be? Some people were always the princesses, never the frogs!

I almost didn't hear Mrs. White say that

Max, the wise giant, would be played by Gregory Greene. I was happy for Gregory, but I couldn't manage a smile.

"I would like to thank everyone who tried out for the major parts," Mrs. White continued. "As you all know, there are other roles in the play. These are the roles of the trees. The saplings, the weeping willows, and the oaks. Tina and I would like all of the children who tried out for the play to have these roles. The saplings will be played by first graders. The weeping willows will be played by third and fourth graders, and the oaks will be played by the fifth graders. Although the trees don't have speaking roles, they are a very important part of the play."

Then Mrs. White read the names of the kids who would play the parts of trees. She must have said my name, but I didn't hear it. I had my hands over my ears. I didn't want to hear anything else. A couple of kids gave me strange looks. I didn't care!

When school was over, I grabbed my books and dashed out of the room. I didn't care what people thought or how I looked. I didn't even care about finding Tina's good-luck charm. All I could think about was how bad I felt.

A tree? A tree!

STEP #5:
Remember:
One Push + One Shove
= Trouble!

By the time I got on the bus, I was sad instead of mad. It was hard to be happy for Betty and Booker when I saw them.

"Congratulations, you two. I'm so glad you're going to be cute little elves," I managed to say.

"Thanks, Willie," said Betty.

"What about you, Willie? Are you going to be Tara, the proud fairy princess?" asked Booker.

I didn't say anything. I just looked out the window. I guess he hadn't heard that Lilac Starr, not me, was going to be playing the part of Tara. Mrs. Cotton, our babysitter, didn't make things any easier when I got home.

"Remember to wipe your feet, Little Thomases. Don't forget to wash your hands if you pet the little animal."

"His name is Doofus Doolittle," I snapped back.

"No candy today, only fruit!" Mrs. Cotton said as she snatched away the cookie I'd saved from my lunch and handed me and Tina apples.

"Yes, Mrs. Cotton," Tina said in the cheerful voice she pulls out when she wants to get on Mrs. Cotton's good side. She could tell I was feeling bad, and she didn't want me to say anything that would get me in trouble. Sometimes my sister really looks out for me.

And then there are those other times.

When Mrs. Cotton went into the kitchen, Tina squeezed down beside me on the couch. She took a big bite of her apple. Still thinking about my cookie, I took a small bite of mine.

"I'm really sorry you didn't get the part, Willie," Tina said.

"But why didn't I get it, Tina? What happened?" I felt like crying. I hoped Tina couldn't tell.

"Willie, do you really want me to tell you the truth, even though it will hurt your feelings?"

"I can take it." After the day I'd had, I thought I could take just about anything. Boy, was I wrong!

"Well, Willie, Lilac Starr was just *better* than you," she said.

"What do you mean, *better* than me?" Considering how well I know my sister, that was a dumb thing to ask.

"Well, Lilac acted just like a real princess," Tina said. "Lilac held her head high, just like a real princess. She walked across the stage, just like a real princess. She threw the cape over her shoulders, just like a real princess. She did everything *just like a real princess*!"

"But I knew all the princess's lines," I said. "I knew everybody's lines!"

Tina gave a long, exaggerated sigh. "I hate to bring this up, Willie, but do you remember what happened yesterday?"

Suddenly the whole miserable experience came back to me in Technicolor. Leave it to Tina to add the sound effects.

"Well, you were the worst person who tried out. You mumbled your lines like you had marbles in your mouth. You stumbled onto the stage like you were walking in your sleep. You—"

"Crawford pushed me onto the stage!" I said in a small voice.

Tina continued as if she hadn't heard me. "You had your eyes closed practically the whole time. Everybody felt sorry for you. If you hadn't been my sister, I—"

"Shut up! I've heard enough!" I said, putting my hands over my ears.

"Well, you wanted to know, and I told you," Tina said with a shrug.

"You're just being mean," I said.

"Well, I'm sorry your feelings are hurt," Tina said, taking another bite out of her apple. "But that's what happened."

"I know you, Tina. You're not really sorry!" I said.

"Think what you want. But look on the bright side: at least you'll be a tree!" Tina picked up the remote and turned on the TV.

Maybe it was because the cartoon characters were laughing when I was feeling sad. Maybe it was because my feelings were hurt, and my sister just didn't care. Maybe it was just one more bad thing on a bad day. All I know is that I gave Tina such a hard push, she fell off the couch. She looked surprised, then got up and shoved me back as hard as she could. I shoved her again. She shoved me back and added a slap on my leg. I slapped her leg and added a punch on her arm. And before we knew it, we were in a fight!

"Stop, Little Thomases! Stop! Stop! Stop!" Mrs. Cotton yelled, running into the living room and waving her hands in the air. "Well, I never! I never! I never!" If Tina and I hadn't been so angry at each other, it would have made us giggle. "You! Go to your father's study! Now!" she said as she grabbed Tina by the arm and led her to the stairs. Then she turned to me. "You! Go to your bedroom! Right this moment!" she said, pointing toward the stairs. "And neither of you can come down until your parents get home!"

Tina and I didn't look at each other as we headed off in different directions. I already felt bad about the fight. Maybe Tina really hadn't meant to hurt my feelings. Maybe she had just told me the truth, like she said. It wasn't her fault that I didn't get the part.

I tried to sneak a look at her to let her know I was sorry, but she was staring straight ahead. So I stared straight ahead, too. When she got to my father's study, she slammed the door closed. I slammed the bedroom door, too.

Tina got the better deal. There was a TV in my dad's study. I heard her turn it on. All I had was my backpack. I hadn't even brought my apple. I fished around in my backpack to see if I could find something interesting to do. There was nothing except my homework, and I didn't feel like studying. Finally, I opened my journal and started to write.

Today stinks! I'm stuck in my crummy room. I didn't get the part of Tara, the proud fairy princess. I lost Tina's good-luck charm. It wasn't on my sweater where I pinned it. I started a fight, and now Tina is mad at me. But she's really going to be mad when she finds out what I did!

Mrs. Cotton was gone by the time my

dad called me and Tina downstairs for dinner. I could tell by the scowl on his face that he was angry at us for fighting. Afterward my mom called us into the living room for a family meeting. Neither of my parents was smiling.

"Your father and I have decided to put you both on punishment for a week and a half for what happened this afternoon," my mom said.

"But Willie started it because I told her the truth about why she didn't get the part in the play!" Tina said.

All I could do was pout. My mom looked at me, then sighed.

"Willie, I'm very sorry that you didn't get the part in the play, but that is no reason to fight," she said. Then she looked at Tina. "I don't care who started it, Tina.

You're old enough to know better and understand how disappointed Willie must have been."

Neither of us said anything. Doofus Doolittle jumped into my lap and licked my chin. I could tell he was trying to make me feel better. I gave him a hug. Then he jumped down and ran over to Tina. He rubbed against her leg. Tina picked him up and hugged him, too.

"There will be no TV while you are on punishment," my dad said. "When you come home from school, Tina, you will go to my study, and Willie, you will go to your room."

"But that's not fair!" I said. "There is a TV in your study, and Tina's going to watch it!"

Tina gave me one of her meanest stares.

If looks could kill, I would have been dead meat.

"I'll take the TV out of my study, and both of you can read or do homework until dinner," my dad said. "Maybe in a week and a half the two of you will appreciate each other's company. Maybe then you'll both understand how *lucky* you are to be sisters."

Why did he have to say *that* word!

"Tell Willie I want my lucky charm back," Tina said. "Willie borrowed it, and she still has it."

My mom and dad looked at me for an answer.

"It's still in school," I said, avoiding everybody's eyes.

Well, that *was* the truth. I just didn't know where in school it was!

STEP #6:
Make Sure Your Costume Annoys the Stuck-up Star

Lucky for me, Tina was so busy worrying about her play over the next week and a half, she only asked about her lucky charm once.

"I'm so-o-o sorry, Tina. It's still in school!" I said, stirring my oatmeal. I couldn't look her in the eye.

"And just when do you plan to bring it home?" She gulped down her juice.

"Soon."

"You'd better. I'll need it Friday for

opening night. Don't you dare forget it again!"

That was on Monday. All I could do was hope for the best. I had been checking the Lost and Found every morning. Whenever I walked down the halls, I looked down at the floor. Nothing had turned up. Sooner or later I'd have to face the music.

Each morning, Mrs. Sweetly asked Crawford and Lilac to tell the class how rehearsals had gone the day before. Crawford talked about how much he loved to act, and how nervous he was about opening night. Lilac told us how excited she was, and that she couldn't wait to wear the beautiful costume.

I also heard about the play at dinner. Every night, Tina told my mom and dad the good and bad things that had happened during rehearsal. Lilac and Crawford were doing good jobs, she said, and she was proud of all the little elves. But she was worried about Bill Taylor, Crawford's understudy. He hadn't learned his lines yet.

"What will happen if Crawford gets sick and can't go on?" she asked my mom in a worried voice.

"Try not to worry about things before they happen," my mom said. "Everything will turn out fine, you'll see!"

"Think positive!" I said, which made Tina smile. It was great to see my sister smiling at me. I really missed talking and laughing with her. Being on punishment for a week and a half was really rotten. When we came home from school, we went our separate ways. Tina took her homework into dad's study. I took mine into our bedroom. Tina was working hard on her play, so she always took her bath first and was usually asleep by the time I took my bath. In the morning, Tina looked over her notes about her play. I talked to Doofus Doolittle. On the bus, Tina talked to Betty, Booker, or Crawford Mills about rehearsals. I gazed out the window.

The week went by quickly. Before I knew it, it was Thursday, the day before opening night. On Friday afternoon, there would be a dress rehearsal before the whole school. Everybody, including us, the trees, would get to wear our costumes. Friday night was the big one. That was the night everyone's parents would come. Our principal had even invited the superintendent of schools. Even the teachers were excited.

Thursday morning, Mrs. White made an

announcement over the PA system.

"Now is the time for the trees to join the play rehearsal," she said. "I want all children who will play trees to come to the auditorium after lunch."

There were twelve kids who were playing

trees. Three first graders were saplings. Three fifth graders were oaks. The rest of us were weeping willows.

When the trees joined the other actors onstage, Mrs. White said she had marked the spots where she wanted us to stand with an X. Each X had our name printed on it. The saplings would sit cross-legged on the fake grass in front of the actors. The oaks would stand in the back with their arms—excuse me—limbs crossed in front of them. The weeping willows were placed around Tara, the proud fairy princess, and Igor, the mean, evil prince. We were the only trees who would move. We would sway to the left and right, on cue. There were two rows of weeping willows. One row stood right next to the princess and prince. The others stood closer to the oaks.

I searched for the X with my name written on it and found it in the front row next to Tara, the proud fairy princess, otherwise known as Lilac Starr.

"You're standing too close to me," Lilac said when I took my place beside her.

"But this is where Mrs. White put my X," I explained, glancing down at my feet to make sure. I was standing directly on top of it. Anybody could see that.

"I don't care where your X is, you have to move back," Lilac said.

"Why?"

"Because the audience won't be able to see my face."

"What makes you think the audience wants to see *your* face?" asked Miles Washington, who was one of the oaks. He lived two streets down from me. Kids from our neighborhood always stand up for each other. He was standing behind me and gave me a grin and a wink when I turned around.

"Because I'm the star of this play!" Lilac said with a proud shake of her head.

"But, Lilac, what makes you think people won't be able to see you?" I tried to sound polite, even though I wasn't feeling that way.

"Have you *seen* your costume yet?"

I could tell by her voice I probably didn't *want* to see it.

"Well, it's covered with disgusting, crepe-paper leaves that go all over the place. When you move they will probably hit me in the face. I have allergies. The dust they stir up might make me sneeze! So move back more!" she said with a wave of her hand.

"Okay." I took another step back. I sure didn't want to make anybody sneeze.

"Not far enough! You have to leave room for your leaves."

This time, I moved back so far I bumped into Miles. That was when he spoke his fateful words.

"Trees are more important to the earth than grouchy fairy princesses," he said to one of the other oaks. "Trees should be the stars! Trees rule the world!" The other fifth graders laughed and gave each other high fives.

Lilac threw them all mean looks. "Mind your own business. And anyway, trees are *never* stars!" She turned back to me. "You're still standing too close, Willie."

This time I stood my ground. "I am *not* moving again!"

69

"Mrs. White!" Lilac raised her hand and waved it to get Mrs. White's attention. "Could you come here for a moment, please!"

Mrs. White came onstage. "What's wrong, Lilac?" Mrs. White looked like she had a lot on her mind. I felt bad that Lilac was bothering her with this.

"Willie is too close to me. Her costume's going to be big and clumsy. I'm afraid she will bump into me, and the audience won't hear me speak."

Mrs. White glanced at the X on the floor. Then she looked back at Lilac. Then she looked at me.

"You're okay, Willie. Just stay where you are," she said, shaking her head as she rushed off the stage.

The problem was, I didn't know whether

she meant "Just stay where you are" *before* or *after* Lilac ordered me to move!

Since it was the day before dress rehearsal, and some of the actors still didn't know their lines, Mrs. White didn't take much time with the trees. She sent us back to our classrooms early.

"You all will do fine," Mrs. White said. "You know where to stand and when to sway, and that's enough. I'll see you tomorrow at the dress rehearsal. Come early so you can get into your costumes!"

That night, Tina was still awake when I got in my bed. She had a frown on her face, and I could tell she was worried. "What if my play doesn't go well tomorrow? What if everything goes wrong?"

"Think positive!"

"Willie, did you forget the good-luck charm again? I really need it now," she said after a couple of minutes. She didn't sound angry or sad, just worried. I pulled the covers over my head and pretended to be asleep.

STEP #7:
Dream of Being a Star

I should know by now that when I dream that something good will happen, something else is on the way. For example, a while back when I dreamed that Doofus Doolittle was playing chopsticks on the piano, the pet show Tina and I were planning turned into a disaster. When I dreamed about catching the biggest fish in the river, I ended up ruining my dad's fishing trip.

In my dream on Thursday night, I was the star of *The Terrific Tale of Tara, the*

Proud Fairy Princess. Miles kept shouting, "Trees rule the world!" and people were clapping and cheering for me. Betty and Booker were jumping up and down. The sixth graders were giving each other high fives. Even Crawford Mills and Lilac Starr

were applauding. I woke up with a smile on my face.

The day started out great. Doofus Doolittle licked my nose as soon as I opened my eyes. I wore my star earrings, green-and-orange skirt, and lucky red socks. Tina was already at breakfast when I came downstairs. My dad was going to drive her to school early because she needed to help Mrs. White get ready for the dress rehearsal.

"Tina, you're the greatest!" I yelled out as she went through the door. It was best not to say the words *good luck*. They might remind her of her good-luck charm.

Tina turned around and grinned. "You're the greatest too, Willie. See you at school." It was just like old times.

My dad had made his special pancakes for breakfast because it was a special day. My mom sat across from me as I finished eating. "Your dad and I are so proud of you and Tina," she said as she drank her coffee. "When we pick you up after the show tonight, we're going to go out to dinner. How does pizza sound?"

"Great!" I said. "Can we get ice cream afterward?"

"Anything you two want," my mom said.

I smiled all the way to the bus. I could almost taste the tomato sauce.

But I had the rest of the day to get through.

The big dress rehearsal was starting at two. Everyone in the whole school was going to be there. All the kids in the play were nervous, even me, although all I had to do was stand and sway. At 1 P.M. Mrs. White's voice came over the PA system.

"All children playing trees, please report to the auditorium for your costumes at once," she said.

Lilac Starr and Crawford Mills had received their costumes several days before. They had been in the auditorium rehearsing since morning.

Lilac's words about my costume concerned me. I was worried as I walked into the auditorium.

All the trees wore brown pants or tights, which were supposed to look like tree trunks. The saplings wore big floppy hats covered with paper leaves. The oaks had green top hats and paper leaves attached to their sleeves. The weeping willows had the best costumes of all. We wore big sheets that reached below our knees. Coming out of our heads were long, thin, strips of paper that were cut to look like the long, dripping branches of willow trees. When we swayed back and forth, the paper made a swishing sound, just like willow leaves blowing in the wind.

"This is great!" said one of the weeping willows as he swayed back and forth.

"Sure is!" I said. I waved my arms up and down. I loved the way the leaves sounded.

"All actors take deep breaths and get

ready. Princess Tara, Prince Igor, Elves, Giant. That means you!" Mrs. White yelled.

Everyone could hear the audience filing into the auditorium. It was weird being behind the curtain and listening to kids laughing and talking as they came in. One of the elves began to cry.

"Stage fright!" whispered Gregory Greene—Max the wise giant.

"He'd better get over it!" said Lilac Starr.

"Trees, take your places, now!" Mrs. White yelled.

I caught a glimpse of Tina talking to Crawford Mills. Crawford kept putting his hand around his throat. Then I saw Tina talking to Bill Taylor and, finally, to Mrs. White. When Tina saw me, she waved. This was my sister's big day and I was really happy for her.

"Get ready, weeping willows!" Mrs. White said. She had told us not to cover our faces until we stood on our Xs. We all put our hoods over our heads, followed by the paper leaves.

We all held our breath. We all were very quiet. The CD began to play over the loud-speaker. There was a hush in the audience. Slowly the curtain began to rise.

First Gregory Greene, Max the wise giant, walked across the stage. The cute little elves scampered around him. I knew that Booker and Betty were nervous, but they were doing the best that they could. I wished that there was a way I could tell them. Crawford, Prince Igor, came onstage next. His lines were the first words spoken in the play. Crawford's voice sounded scratchy, as if he might have a sore throat, but nobody seemed to notice.

Then Lilac, Tara the proud fairy princess, came onstage. The audience gasped in amazement!

"Wow! What a beautiful dress!" I heard somebody say.

"I wish I could be her," another kid said.

Lilac held her head very high. She stepped in tiny, dainty steps as she took her place. But when she saw me on my X, she narrowed her eyes and poked out her mouth. I knew then there was going to be trouble.

STEP #8:
Quit Dreaming—
You're a Tree!

"Move back!" Lilac said out of the side of her mouth. She spoke in a whisper. A *loud* whisper.

"I'm standing on my X," I whispered back.

She turned to face the audience. "I am Tara, the proud fairy princess!"

Gregory—Max the wise giant—bowed.

The audience applauded.

"You are proud, but are you wise?" Max asked Tara.

"And who are you?" Tara asked Igor, the mean, evil prince.

"I am Igor. I will soon be king of all the land!"

Then it was the cute little elves' turn. They skipped around the stage. Then they began to dance. Lilac looked back at me.

"Move it!" she said out of the corner of her mouth.

"Mrs. White told me to stay where I was, and that's what I'm doing," I said in a low voice.

Lilac turned her attention back to the play.

"I am Igor, the great prince. I have strength. You have none!" Crawford said. His voice sounded as if it hurt him to talk.

"But I command the woods and forests!"

Princess Tara said to Prince Igor.

That was the cue for me and the other weeping willows to sway. When I moved to the left, Lilac stepped on my right toe. Hard.

"Ouch!" I said.

"Your leaves hit me in the face!" Lilac said under her breath.

"I'm on my X, and don't you dare step on my toe again!" I said.

One of the saplings giggled. I hoped the audience hadn't heard us, too.

"We are all visitors in this beautiful forest," said Max, the wise giant. "It doesn't belong to any of us. Nobody can own the trees."

That was the cue for the weeping willows to shake our arms so our leaves would flutter.

But when I shook my arm, my leaves
hit Lilac in the face.

"Achoo!" she sneezed. "Achoo! Achoo!
Achoo! Your leaves are making me sneeze!"
she said.

"Sorry!" I whispered, stepping away from

her so my leaves wouldn't get in her face.

That was a big mistake!

"Hey, did you see that! That tree is walking!" somebody shouted from the audience.

"Hey, the tree walked. The tree walked!"

"Yeah, trees rule the earth!" one of the sixth graders yelled. Some kids in the front row heard him, and they started chanting, "Trees rule the earth! Trees rule the earth!"

"Get back!" Lilac whispered to me. I stepped back as far as I could.

"Hey, that tree walked again!" somebody said.

"Go, tree! Go, tree! Go, tree!" a bunch of kids started yelling.

"Trees rule the earth!" somebody yelled out again.

Lilac sneezed so hard her crown fell off her head.

Suddenly everybody in the audience was laughing. A couple of sixth graders started to whistle.

I stood perfectly still and held my breath. What was going to happen next?

Mrs. Morris, the principal, jumped out of her seat and rushed to the front of the room. She stood in front of the stage and clapped her hands six times. Then she put her hands on her hips and stared hard at every kid who was laughing.

"There will be order in this room! There will be order in this room!" she said.

Everybody stopped laughing. Everybody was quiet. Nobody wanted to cross Mrs. Morris. Even the sixth graders behaved.

"This play will continue!" she said. Then she sat back down.

The next line belonged to Prince Igor. But when Crawford opened his mouth to speak, his voice was so scratchy you couldn't hear what he was saying.

"Crawford, speak louder!" Mrs. White whispered from the wings. His voice came out in a croak.

Then the giggles started. When one person starts, the giggles jump from one person to the next. And that's what happened. The elves began to giggle. Then the giggles hopped to the saplings, and nothing could make them stop. Then the oaks. And the willows.

Finally, the play was over. The audience applauded. I guess they'd had a good time. But we were just glad to see the curtain come down. The moment it hit the floor, Tina came running on stage.

"My play is ruined!" she screamed. Then she glared at me.

"Willie, if you had moved back when Lilac told you to, then Lilac wouldn't have started sneezing, and the elves wouldn't have started giggling, and—" She put her hands over her face.

I looked down at the floor. Tina was right. Why hadn't I just done what Lilac said?

After the audience had left the auditorium, Mrs. White called us all together. She told us to sit in a circle.

"What happened today was nobody's fault," she said. "Yesterday, I really didn't take the time to explain to Willie where she should stand. She stood where her X was, which was the right thing to do. And Lilac didn't mean to sneeze. She couldn't help it."

"The elves and saplings shouldn't have giggled!" said Gregory Greene.

"I think the audience thought that was part of the play," Mrs. White said. "Sometimes things happen in a play that you can't control. But as long as it works, it's okay." Everyone laughed at that. Maybe things hadn't been as bad as they seemed.

"This afternoon was only a dress rehearsal. We have a saying in theater that a bad dress rehearsal always means a great opening night. I'm sure that's what will happen tonight."

Everybody was feeling a little bit better. Maybe Mrs. White was right. Even Tina looked relieved.

"So we're going to run through the play, from beginning to end, one last time, and then we'll all be ready for opening night. But first take the hand of the person sitting next to you," Mrs. White said.

Gregory was sitting on one side of me

and Booker was on the other. It felt strange holding hands with Booker and Gregory, but it made me feel strong, too.

"Now, we're going to go around the circle, and every one of you is going to say these words: We are a team!"

"We are a team!" said Tina.

"We are a team!" said Betty.

"We are a team!" said Lilac.

Then it was Crawford Mills's turn to speak. When he opened his mouth, no words came out.

STEP #9:
Forget Step #8. Fairy Tales Always Have Happy Endings!

We all stared at Crawford.

"Are you all right?" Mrs. White asked.

"I can't talk!" Crawford squeaked.

Mrs. White told one of the sixth graders to run to the nurse's office to get Mrs. Lois, our school nurse. When she came into the auditorium, she rushed to Crawford and placed her hand on his forehead.

"Oh, my goodness!" she said, snatching

her hand off Crawford's head. "You have a high fever. You're burning up!"

Crawford moved his lips. Mrs. Lois bent down to hear what he said. She looked up at Mrs. White.

"This boy is sick!" she said. "He's hot and he has a sore throat. I'm going to call his mother to come and get him right away!'

"No-o-o-o!" said Crawford.

"Yes!" said Mrs. Lois.

Mrs. Lois looked at Mrs. White. They both looked at Crawford. Mrs. White shook her head. "This is bad news," she said in a low voice.

Crawford and Mrs. Lois left for her office so that she could call his mother. The rest of us just stood there.

Lilac threw up her hands. "Just my luck!" she said.

"*Your* luck? What about poor Crawford? He's the one who has a fever. He's the one who is sick!" said Gregory.

"What are we going to do now?" asked Booker.

"Bill, I think it might be up to you," said Mrs. White.

We all looked at Bill Taylor. He was the person who was supposed to play Prince Igor if Crawford was sick. Now the play depended on him.

Bill looked scared. He looked worried. He stared down at his feet.

"Bill?" Mrs. White said in a quiet voice.

"I don't know the lines," Bill said. "I wasn't paying attention. I didn't think Crawford was going to be sick. I don't know what to do."

"Are you willing to try to do the part?" Mrs. White asked.

Bill nodded that he was. But he still looked worried.

Mrs. White gave a long sigh. I glanced at Tina. She looked like she was about to cry.

"Everybody ready? Let's start our rehearsal now," said Mrs. White.

We all got into our places. Bill said the first few lines of the play. But then he had to read the script. He sounded like he was reading a story instead of speaking the lines. He didn't *act* like Prince Igor. Everyone tried very hard to do their parts right. Everybody did what they were supposed to do. Except for Bill Taylor. I felt sorry for him. Prince Igor was a really important character. The play didn't work without him.

When we finished, nobody said anything.

I looked around for Tina. She was sitting in the last row in the auditorium. Even though I couldn't see her face, I knew how sad she must feel.

"Bill, I think you will have to read from the script tonight," Mrs. White said. Then she turned toward the rest of us. "Before the play opens, I'll go out and explain to the audience that one of our lead characters suddenly took ill, and his understudy will read his part. Come on, everybody, let's get out of our costumes, and I'll see everybody back here in time for our performance tonight." She tried to sound cheerful, but her face didn't look that way.

"What do you mean Bill is going to read from the script?" Lilac asked.

"Just what I said, Lilac," said Mrs. White.

"That's going to sound dumb!" one of the first graders said.

"Everybody is going to laugh at us!" said Betty.

"This is going to be *so* embarrassing," said Lilac.

I felt sorry for Bill, but I couldn't think of anything to say that would make him feel better.

"Let's not do it. Let's postpone it until Crawford comes back!" said one of the fifth graders.

"It's too late to postpone it," said Mrs. White. "The notices have all gone out. Everybody is coming tonight. It's perfectly fine for an understudy to take over for one of the stars. It happens all the time in the theater."

"Yeah, but the understudy always

knows his lines!" Gregory said.

"It's going to throw off the whole play!" said Lilac. Bill looked like he was going to cry.

"That's enough, everybody!" Mrs. White said.

"Tina, what do you think we should do?" Gregory asked.

Slowly, Tina walked to the front of the room and climbed up on the stage. I have never felt as sorry for her as I did then.

"Everything is wrong," she said in a small voice. "Bill doesn't know his lines. It's not his fault; he didn't know that Crawford was going to get sick all of a sudden. Everybody laughed during the dress rehearsal because Willie moved and Lilac sneezed. Maybe we should just forget the whole thing!"

I came over to Tina and put my arm around her.

"Don't feel bad, Tina. This is a really good play," I said.

"But nobody will know it!" she said. "This will be the last play I'll ever write!"

"You can't just give up!"

"Who says?"

"I say!"

"Why not?"

"Because I can play the part of Prince Igor!" There was somebody else who knew Igor's lines. And that somebody was me!

"But you're a girl!" said Lilac.

"Who cares!" said Gregory.

"I know all the lines that Crawford has to say," I said. "I know what he has to do.

I'll tie up my braids and tuck them under my crown!"

"I don't want to be the princess if Willie Thomas is going to be the prince," sniffed Lilac.

"That's great, because I know *your* lines too!" said Ruby, Lilac's understudy.

"Okay! I guess I'll be the princess," said Lilac.

"Don't do us any favors. Even princesses can be replaced," said Gregory. He picked up Prince Igor's crown and placed it on my head. "I crown you Prince Igor!"

Everybody applauded, and Tina smiled a bright, wide, happy smile. Mrs. White gave me a pat on the back. "Come on, kids, let's give it another try!" she said.

Crawford's costume was too big, so Mrs. White took it home to wash it and take it in for me. Lilac was taller than me, but who said a prince has to be taller than a princess? The rehearsal that afternoon was great, and opening night was even better. It was fun saying Igor's lines. I hadn't noticed it before, but he had the best lines in the play. They got the most laughs.

The audience gave us four curtain calls, and Mrs. Morris presented Tina with a big bouquet of pink and red roses. I was really proud to be Igor, even though I wasn't listed in the program. The best, though, was yet to come.

When I took my bow, I spotted something in a shiny plastic case near the lights in the front of the stage. You guessed it! It was Tina's good-luck charm, waiting to be discovered. As soon as the curtain dropped, I picked it up and gave it to Tina.

"You lost it, didn't you?" She peered at me as if she were reading my mind.

"Yeah. I didn't want to tell you because I was afraid you'd be mad at me."

"I *am* mad that you lost my lucky charm," Tina said, then grinned. "But you saved my play and you're the only sister I've got, so I have to forgive you." She divided her bouquet of flowers and gave half to me.

"For a good frog, a better prince, and the very best sister in the whole, wide world!" Tina said with a bow. Then she grabbed my hand and off we ran to find our mom and dad.

Tina and I ate three slices of pizza each! That's the most we've ever eaten at one time. There were only two slices to bring home. Tina was glad to have her lucky charm back. I was glad she had it too, since it only brought me BAD luck. The next week, the school newspaper interviewed Tina about the play. I copied down my favorite part: "Willimena Thomas, my sister and a third grader in Mrs. Sweetly's class, saved the school play when she stood in for Crawford Mills, the evil prince, who was sent home sick." Can you believe Tina said that? I guess fairy tales really do have happy endings and frogs still turn into princes! So, back off, Lilac Starr—there's a new star at Harriet Tubman, and her name is WILLIMENA!

Willie

P.S.: So sunny skies are here again! But my scariest holiday is on the horizon—and it's not Halloween. Would you believe . . . Valentine's Day!?!

Why does Valentine's Day give Willie the creeps? Read all about it in . . .

WILLIMENA RULES!
23 Ways to Mess Up Valentine's Day
Rule Book #5